This Topsy and Tim book belongs to

_____

Topsy and Tim Play Football

By Jean and Gareth Adamson

Illustrations by Belinda Worsley

A catalogue record for this book is available from the British Library

Published by Ladybird Books Ltd
A Penguin Company
Penguin Books Ltd., 80 Strand, London WC2R 0RL, UK
Penguin Books Australia Ltd., Camberwell, Victoria, Australia
Penguin Group (NZ) 67 Apollo Drive, Rosedale, North Shore 0632, New Zealand

002 –
3 5 7 9 10 8 6 4 2

ISBN: 978-1-40930-335-0
Printed in China

www.topsyandtim.com

Topsy and Tim were getting dressed for
football club in the park.
"My shirt doesn't fit," said Tim.
"Because it's back to front," said Topsy.

At last they were ready to go. Dad was going with them.
"Have you got our drinks?" asked Tim
"They're in my rucksack," said Dad.

Kerry and Tony and little Stevie Dunton
were on their way to football club, too.
"Hi, Topsy and Tim," they called.

Soon they joined a group of children in the park.
All of them were wearing football shirts and trainers.

"Good morning everyone," said Les, their football instructor. "Let's start with a run, to warm us up."

The children lined up behind Les and
ran to the far side of the park and back.

"I'm lovely and hot now," panted Tim.
"I need a drink," puffed Topsy.
All the children were hot and thirsty after the run.
Luckily the mums and dads had got bottles of cool
water for everyone.

"Now we'll learn some football skills," said Les. The children had to run in and out of a row of cones, as quickly as possible. "Well done, Topsy," said Les.

Next, they did the same thing backwards.
That was not at all easy. Tim tripped up.
"Whoops!" he said.

"You all did well," said Les. "Now I want you to do the same again, dribbling your footballs along as you go."

"My baby brother is a good dribbler," joked Tony.

The children worked hard at dribbling their footballs in and out of the cones. At last Les blew his whistle for them to stop.

"I think you are ready for a real game of football now," he said.

"HOORAY!" shouted the children.

Les had brought red and blue bibs for the children to wear. Dad helped Topsy and Tim to put theirs on.

Les split the children into two teams, a blue team
and a red team. Tim and Tony were in the blue
team. Topsy and Kerry and little Stevie Dunton
were in the red team.

At last everyone was ready. Les blew his whistle and threw the ball in. Stevie reached it first, gave it a big kick – and sat down with a bump.

Topsy ran after the ball and kicked it to Kerry.
Kerry dribbled it past John, past Tim, past Tony,
past Justin – and right off the pitch.

Les threw the ball back in. Tony kicked it to
John. John kicked it to Justin. Justin passed it
back to Tim – and Tim scored the first goal!
Everybody cheered – and the game went on.

Soon lots of goals had been scored, and it was
nearly time to stop. The red team needed just one
more goal to make it even.
"Come on the reds!" shouted Kerry's dad.
But Justin, in the blue team, chased the ball and
kicked it high up in the air…

The ball came down, landed on Topsy's head with a BOMP – and bounced off, straight into the goal. Everyone laughed and cheered.

Les blew his whistle to end the game.
"Well done all of you," he said.
It was time to go home. Dad wiped the worst of
the mud off the twins and their footballs.

"I can see you had a good time," said Mummy
when they reached home.
"I wish we had football club every day," said Tim.

"We could practise in the garden," said
Topsy. And that is exactly what they did.

*Now turn the page and help
Topsy and Tim solve a puzzle.*

Topsy, Tim and Kerry have each kicked a football.
Where did each ball go?
Who scored a goal?

BOMP

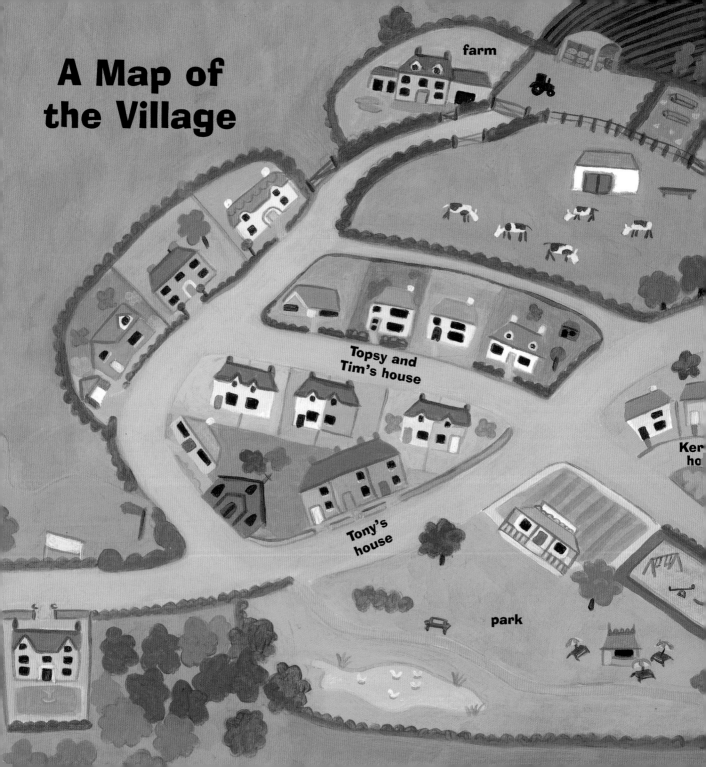

A Map of the Village

farm

Topsy and
Tim's house

Tony's
house

Ker
ho

park

garage

post office

health centre

church

primary school

nursery school

police station

Look out for other titles in the series.

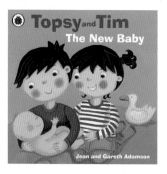

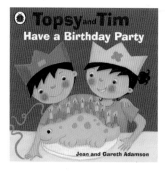

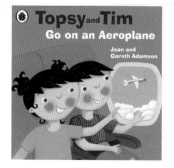

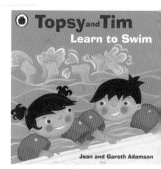

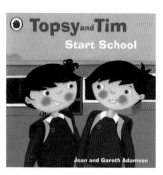

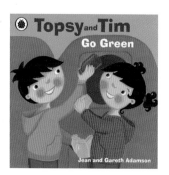

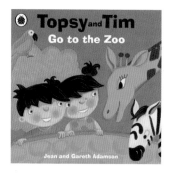

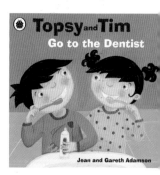

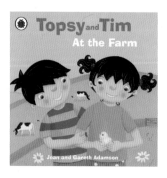

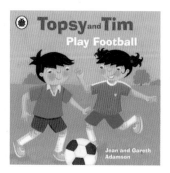